# MINI SAGAS

## Creative Capers

THE EAST MIDLANDS
EDITED BY HELEN DAVIES

First published in Great Britain in 2011 by:

 Young**Writers**

Remus House
Coltsfoot Drive
Peterborough
PE2 9BF
Telephone: 01733 890066
Website: www.youngwriters.co.uk

# FOREWORD

Young Writers was established in 1990 with the aim of encouraging and nurturing writing skills in young people and giving them the opportunity to see their work in print. By helping them to become more confident and expand their creative skills, we hope our young writers will be encouraged to keep writing as they grow.

School pupils nationwide have been exercising their minds to create their very own short stories, Mini Sagas, using no more than fifty words, to be included here in our latest competition, *The Adventure Starts Here* ...

The entries we received showed an impressive level of creativity and imagination, providing an absorbing look into the eager minds of our future authors.

# YE CONTENTS OF AUTHORS

Congratulations to all young writers who appear in this book

## Monks' Dyke Technology College, Louth

## Newbridge High School, Coalville

## Portland Comprehensive School, Worksop

## St Benedict Catholic School & Performing Arts College, Derby

## Spalding High School, Spalding

# MINI SAGAS

# GOAL

The clock is at 90 minutes. We are drawing 1-1. I see the fourth official's board go up. The number 2 pops up on it. I make a crunching tackle. I win. I run past the defenders. *Boom!* I shoot past the keeper. The whistle.
Goal!

Josh Maddison (12)

# TRICK OR TREAT?

Night-time - all was quiet. The moon shone in the dark sky, clouds moved, scary faces shown. Wind blew, trees swayed, shadows made.
I heard creaks, door handle moved, reached for the switch - not found! Someone knocked.
'Who's there?'
Opened the door - 'Trick or treat?'

Ruman Johal (16)

# THE RED RING

Since we've found the reason that fits the Red Ring.
It steals into the kingdom, hiding in a rat. Shops are
shut, houses are locked. Parents can stay, children
go. Unbarring the gates of London and turning them
crazy with Red Ring.
'Tishoo, 'tishoo, they all have the plague!

Charlotte Topley
**Farnborough School, Clifton**

# THE WINNER

There he is, panting like a panther. The whistle blows
and he's off! He runs as fast as a cheetah but then,
out of nowhere comes the opposition. They mercilessly
pursue him and then, one slide and he's down.
One last chance to score the winning free kick.

Joseph Linley (13)
**Farnborough School, Clifton**

# THE MOST FAMOUS FACE

She walked down the corridor of Kensington Palace, her sapphire blue wedding ring glistened on her finger. For once in her life she didn't have to face the paparazzi; the flash of the cameras and the lies in the papers.
She smiled, a happy, lonely smile, as she faded away.

Ashley Ellis (12)
**Farnborough School, Clifton**

# WHEN THE WIND BLOWS

She put the baby outside in the arms of Mother Nature. She left her baby to perish in the wind and she left her baby to fall to its death.
No one heard the baby cry for help, nobody went to help, then as the bough broke the baby fell.

Alison Dunnett (12)
**Farnborough School, Clifton**

# THE CHIMNEY CREEP

How I hate that big, fat fella! He started breaking into my house when I was just one! We moved; he followed. He's a stalker!
His sinister, midget gang of nine keep watch and he has a getaway sleigh waiting in the snow.
You should be careful on Christmas Eve ...

Leanne George (12)

**Farnborough School, Clifton**

# CAN'T CATCH ME

He was sprinting in front of animals. His head was high; mocking, laughing, running like the new Bolt! He leapt, as his leg hit the rock, making crumbs. The fresh smell of the man was irresistible for the fox.
When the fox leapt the man crumbled into freshly gingered pieces.

Faizan Shah (13)

**Farnborough School, Clifton**

# BEAST VS ANIMAL

She exited her lair. She walked down the dark alley. She saw something with her red eyes. It was like an eagle was following her. The thing said nothing but growled. It leapt from the shadows, it had sharp teeth and blood dripping from its chin.
I changed into form. *Fight!*

Lewis Shelton (12)
**Farnborough School, Clifton**

# AN OLD FRIEND

I watched my grandad slowly close his eyes as the nurses took him away. A tear ran down my cheek, followed by many more.
That night I faintly saw a ghostly figure, or so I thought. Its pale hands touched mine and its white face smiled.
'Grandad?' I whispered softly ...

Melissa Elvin (12)
**Farnborough School, Clifton**

# THE MAN

He watches you when you sleep. He's the man you can't get away from. Even if you move house, he's still there, watching you!
He drinks alone in the dead of night. He flies across the sky as he visits his other victims!
'Ho, ho, ho,' he says.

Alexander Knight (12)
**Farnborough School, Clifton**

# BIG SCHOOL

Turning the corner, there it was, Big School! I entered, they stared. What do I do? I headed towards form but was blocked by a Year 11. He stared at me. Terrified, I tried to dodge, nothing worked.
'What's your name?'
He was nice. I was safe for now!

Stephanie Danby (11)
**Frederick Gough School, Scunthorpe**

## REALITY'S FANTASY

'Alison,' bellowed her mother, angrily charging into the room like a crazed bull. 'Snap out of it!'
Alison gently opened her eyes, not fazed by her mum's scream. 'Zip it Mum, what's with the shouting? The Shadow's changed, I melted him with butterflies!'
Alison seemed confused, so did her mother.

Abigail Whitelam (11)

**Frederick Gough School, Scunthorpe**

## DEADLY DINNER

He squeezed through the hole. Off he went. Scurrying past pots, pans, knives and forks. Swimming in the pool of gravy before navigating the spice pot skyscrapers. He had nearly completed his mission. There it was - the mothership, the cheese block. It was heavenly.
'Say cheese!'
*Chop* went the knife!

Ben Carpenter (11)

**Frederick Gough School, Scunthorpe**

# SPACESHIP

Twisting and turning in a spaceship; once you're in you can't get out! Screams of terror echoed all around; the fear of approaching death. Ghostly voices cackled, 'You're trapped!'
Unexpectedly a deep, booming voice bellowed loudly, 'Thank you for riding The Spaceship.'
The heavy doors slowly opened!

Laura Sausby (12)

**Frederick Gough School, Scunthorpe**


# UNIQUE CUPBOARD

I stood there, staring silently. *I've been waiting for this for years,* I thought contentedly.
'You look like you were when I was forbidden to see you, look at me now! I studied up and down to check if it really was you.'
Amazingly it was my unique biscuit cupboard!

Claire Smith (11)

**Frederick Gough School, Scunthorpe**

# THE MOUNTAIN MONSTER OF DOOM

The man continuously climbed up the steep, rocky mountainside; constantly slipping back down the high ledge, way above the clouds. There was no worse time to be dehydrated.

As the man carefully approached the top his life flashed before his eyes.

As the mountain monster shouted, 'Wagbo!' he fell.

Lewis Chambers (11)

**Frederick Gough School, Scunthorpe**

# SHIVERS

A man stumbling down the alley, vodka in one hand, knife in the other. He came closer.

'You die tonight!' he screamed as he charged forward.

*Click!* The TV went off.

'I don't like horror films,' said George.

'Yeah, they give me the shivers,' said Ben.

Jamie Clayton (12)

**Frederick Gough School, Scunthorpe**

# DODGE OF DEATH

It came towards me at the speed of light. It was sharp with a pointy end. I covered my face, hoping not to die. I dodged out of the way, but not quickly enough. I laughed as I realised how ridiculous I was being ...
The 3D movie had finally finished.

Emma Stokes (11)

**Frederick Gough School, Scunthorpe**

# WHAT TICKETS?

She was there at last. The place of all places, Disneyland, Florida. She had been waiting forever to be there. She could see the palace, Minnie and Mickey Mouse, the large crowds. She was at the gigantic metal gates.
'Tickets please,' said the man.
Dad replied, 'What tickets?'

Ryan Coulson (12)

**Frederick Gough School, Scunthorpe**

# BANG!

*Bang!* Standing in the middle of a battlefield, Jack felt uncomfortable. He walked along and realised he had a gun and was wearing camouflage. He had to talk to someone, to see what was going on.
He turned around. *Bang!* He collapsed to the floor and *splash* into his dog's bowl!

Liam Barnby (11)

**Frederick Gough School, Scunthorpe**

# A FISHY SNACK

A penguin was searching for a fishy snack. It spotted a large fish-like silhouette under the ice and dived down. Why was this area so empty?
The shape grew as the penguin approached it. Then suddenly the shark turned around and snapped its jaws around the unlucky, hungry penguin.

George Dalton (11)

**Frederick Gough School, Scunthorpe**

# A WRONG TURN

The prince battled through the forest to get to the captured princess. He chopped, slashed and wrestled with the trees. He paused as he noticed a price tag on a tree. He must have taken a wrong turn in the land of make-believe; he was in a garden centre!

Lewis Bowness (12)

**Frederick Gough School, Scunthorpe**

# THE THING

Glowing eyes stared at me. A smell of rotting flesh filled my nostrils, stinging them. Razor teeth were attached to a mangled mouth.
It pounced forward, towards me. Then I heard it, pounding feet outside. The creature wasn't trying to kill me, it was running away from the thing outside.

Casey Nicholls (11)

**Frederick Gough School, Scunthorpe**

# THE HAIR PARLOUR

I was forced in with a push from my mum! She said to the evil woman standing behind me, 'He'll need strapping in or he'll run!'
There was no escaping! She began, I had a three on top and two on the sides.
All my golden locks had gone forever.

Paul Guntrip (12)
**Frederick Gough School, Scunthorpe**

# CHAOS

I banged on the door loudly, but no one answered. I quickly ran to the place it all happened. I saw my mum in the middle of all the chaos. I ran over to her so I could tell her about it, but she already knew I was dead!

Mayzie Rusiecki (11)
**Frederick Gough School, Scunthorpe**

# THE DREAM

Jeff was walking along the Alps when he slipped on the vertical mountain ... The next thing he knew he was falling rapidly into darkness. Quicker and quicker he went. Jeff jumped and looked around him, there was nothing there.
'What was I thinking! It was just a dream!'

Liam Everitt (11)

**Frederick Gough School, Scunthorpe**

# CONCENTRATION

The atmosphere was awesome, everyone was cheering when I glanced over to my friend in the crowd.
Suddenly a fist appeared across my face. I reacted instinctively and threw the fastest punch ... Seconds later I found my opponent lying flat on the floor, with depression of loss. Victory was mine!

James Balk (12)

**Frederick Gough School, Scunthorpe**

# SHARK ATTACK

There it was, staring me in the eye, the great white shark. I made as much movement as possible. It approached me, it got closer and closer. Then ... *bang!* All I saw that day was a squashed up face of a great white shark on the window of the aquarium.

Ryan Alderson (11)

**Frederick Gough School, Scunthorpe**

# THE WORST DAY EVER

She rushed home, swung the door open, ran upstairs, dropped her bags and jumped onto her bed. Tears started streaming down her face whilst she was punching her pillow; she wished she could stop them.

*Today has been the worst day ever,* she thought - wishing she had never been born ...

Katie Dennett (11)

**Frederick Gough School, Scunthorpe**

# MY FIRST DAY AT NURSERY

Everything looked so big. The sun was shining brightly. I could feel it on my back, through the double doors. As I walked inside I saw more toys than I could ever want in my life! The floor was soft and comfy. Nursery may not be so bad after all!

Olivia Cunningham (14)

**Friar Gate House School, Derby**


# LAST TIME

I looked down at the cliff I had just climbed and thought about the first time I ascended it. It had been a warm, sunny day then, as it was now. I turned and walked from the valley, my home, for what I knew would be the last time.

Jason Mathurin (15)

**Friar Gate House School, Derby**

# UNTITLED

I heard it coming up the stairs. *Boom, boom!* Door handle turning, door opening. *Scratch, creak!* Nothing there; couldn't see anything. Just a dream.
*Boom, boom, scratch, creak!* Definitely something there. *Screech!* My vision was blocked by spiky scales. A moment's fleeting pain, a blinding light, which path to take?

Samuel Phipps (12)

**Lady Manners School, Bakewell**


# KNOCKING NOISE!

I wake up suddenly. *Knock, knock, knock!*
Clambering out of bed, creeping downstairs, heart beating like a drum.
*Knock, knock, knock!* Reaching for the handle, slowly, steadily. I open the door ... Nothing! Suddenly a fur ball leaps up and licks me in pleasure; to say thanks for saving me!

Daymer Eshelby (12)

**Lady Manners School, Bakewell**

# DO I REALLY LIVE IN A MAD HOUSE?

Do I really live in a mad house? I have six brothers, four stepsisters, a dog and a rabbit, my mum, my stepfather and my grandma!
Every single day there's a fight, a disaster, an achievement, a smile, a laugh, a frown, a cry!
I don't think so, do you?

Tiggie Clasper (12)
**Lady Manners School, Bakewell**


# TWO-FACED

Came in from the lake. We sat, we talked, we laughed. Happiness.
But stop, so strange. Must resurface. Blackness, I'm back, my daughter tied to her chair. On her blue lips - painted smile. White eyes glared. I did this.

Sophie Dillon (13)
**Lady Manners School, Bakewell**

## THE PLUMMET TO DOOM

*Bang! Kaboom!* As the aeroplane plummeted to the ground everyone screamed. The plane was falling out of the sky.

When the plane hit the ground everyone jolted forward. There were only a few survivors, not many. They were stranded and who knows how long they would be stuck?

Jessica Lilley

**Lammas School, Sutton-in-Ashfield**

## A DAY IN THE LIFE OF A DEAD FROG

I hop along the lily pads all day. In Heaven they go on forever. It's depressing, occasionally there are skeletal bugs for me to eat. God treats me well but I crave the sweet, fresh air. I know it will never be. That is my story.

Emily Naylor

**Lammas School, Sutton-in-Ashfield**

# LIFE OF A PEN

It's boring being a pen. Someone clicks me, I make contact with paper. I am dropped on the floor, I get trampled on. I talk with other pens in a small, dark pencil case. People throw me in the bin as a laugh. Oh well, at least I hear secrets!

Tara Hill (12)

**Lammas School, Sutton-in-Ashfield**

# GLADIATOR'S BLOOD

They walk out, frightened. The crowd roar as the two brave men meet their perilous doom. All their lives they have been trained for every swing and smash of their swords. They will see who spills blood first.
*Swing!* He is impaled by a sword, the victor has no equal.

Cameron Dhaliwal (13)

**Lammas School, Sutton-in-Ashfield**

# THE SURPRISE

The timer beeped faster and louder. A drop of sweat fell from the man's brow. He pulled and tugged at the wire. It snapped - the beeping grew faster. The man cut a second wire, the timer reached zero. The man waited.
The surprise happened, a clown popped out laughing!

James Keeling (13)

**Lammas School, Sutton-in-Ashfield**

# LOST FREEDOM

John crawled out of his prison cell from the tunnel he'd dug. As he stood outside the prison he felt freedom had come to him.
Suddenly the prison alarms sounded, so he wasted no time and ran for a place to hide. He was spotted.
'Put your hands up!'

Victor Camilleri (13)

**Lammas School, Sutton-in-Ashfield**

# A SUDDEN TRANSFORMATION

Lana lay awake on her bed. Suddenly she heard a swift sound, she was about to lift her head to see what it was when she felt painfully sharp teeth plunge into her neck and blood draining from her.
The pain stopped suddenly. Lana knew she was now ... a vampire.

Gethana Shasitharren (11)
**Leysland High School, Countesthorpe**

# CRACKY THE SUPERHERO

Cracky, the superhero, got a new costume, but he'd lost weight and was too thin! His costume was floppy. He was chasing a criminal but couldn't catch him. He stood on his own floppy costume and tripped.
Cracky flew through the air and landed on the criminal.

Dylan Gold (11)
**Maplewell Hall School, Loughborough**

# HARRY'S HOLIDAY

Harry went on holiday in a caravan. At night it was freaky. The light flashed and turned off. Then he saw a castle and went in. Inside Harry saw a devil! A soldier went to kill Harry and he did!

Liam Shade (11)

**Maplewell Hall School, Loughborough**


# THE CHRISTMAS GHOST

Long ago there was a little girl named Gemma and she used to turn the Christmas lights on.
Then one year, she died, because the plug was wet and it exploded when she turned the lights on.
Another little girl turned on the Christmas lights ... they were haunted!

Jessica Durrant (11)

**Maplewell Hall School, Loughborough**

# THE MYSTERY

There was a ghost house. The girl was scared at the ghost house. The girl went missing. Her mum said to the police, 'She didn't come back! She had on a top and skirt but no shoes.'

The girl was in a cage. There was a boy who rescued her.

Hannah Pollard (11)

**Maplewell Hall School, Loughborough**

# SCARY DOG

A scary dog went to fight another dog that was even scarier. Then they stopped fighting because they were bleeding to death. They were put down.

They went to doggy heaven, they were given lots of toys to play with and lots of things to eat and drink.

Katie Bailiss (11)

**Maplewell Hall School, Loughborough**

# VISIT TO THE DOCTOR'S

Once upon a time there was a little boy. He went home. His mum asked him to go to the doctor's to have an x-ray because he had a broken rib. The doctor put him to sleep and he fixed his rib.
Now he could play.

Ella Toon (11)

**Maplewell Hall School, Loughborough**

# THE HAUNTED HOUSE

There was a haunted house in a scared village. In the village was a little girl called Ella. She went bravely inside the haunted house. She went into the spooky rooms and looked around. The smell was deadly air. She heard footsteps coming towards her - she died.

Emma Mee (11)

**Maplewell Hall School, Loughborough**

# THE MYSTERY

In World War I the soldiers of England were getting ready for the fight.
In the forest the ghost came and cast a spell. All of the weapons disappeared. The soldiers were shocked.

Toby Lloyd (11)

**Maplewell Hall School, Loughborough**

# A DAY IN THE LIFE OF ARMY SPACEMAN SAMUEL PHILIP COOK

My name's Samuel Philip Cook. I'm an army man in space. I shoot the aliens in space and eat them for dinner. I fly around in my rocket visiting all the planets. I live on Planet Earth with my mum, dad and brothers and my dogs called Abbie and Poppy.

Samuel Cook

**Maplewell Hall School, Loughborough**

# THE HAUNTED HOUSE

Me and Spike were walking from a football match when suddenly Spike found an old castle.
I said, 'Do you want to go inside?'
Spike said, 'No.'
'Why?'
'Because it looks scary,' said Spike.
So Spike and I went inside. Then a creak and a crack. We went back out!

Shaun Dakin (15)

**Maplewell Hall School, Loughborough**


# HAUNTED HOUSE

The ghost lives under the bed. He scares people who come into the house by making noises and throwing things around.
Nobody dares to stay there at night and the house becomes old and falls apart.

Jake Hemsley (13)

**Maplewell Hall School, Loughborough**

# A SCHOOLBOY'S TALE

The classroom was loud and noisy. The children broke a window and glass shattered everywhere. The boys were going mad. They were fighting each other. The teachers were angry and the boys were made to clean the whole school.

Tyler O'Gelsby (12)

**Maplewell Hall School, Loughborough**

# FINAL BATTLE

I was very tired. I had been fighting for the last 15 hours against the evil Sage Slash. I hit the bad guy with a huge blow. He had 15 hit points left.

*Whack!* and the enemy suffered a dismal death. But his skeleton came back to haunt me.

Conor Ellis (12)

**Maplewell Hall School, Loughborough**

## SOLDIER VS MAFIA

Jack is in the army and is in a war. Rack is in the Mafia and against the army.
Jack shouted, 'The enemy is here.'
The army gets the nuclear bunker ready to blow up the Mafia! But the buster detonates too soon in the army camp ...

Brandon Lowe 12)

**Maplewell Hall School, Loughborough**

## THE HAUNTED HOUSE

The haunted house sits on top of the hill in the village of Leicester. I arrive and open the door. The house is full of cobwebs and looks spooky. I see a ghost appear at the window. I turn quickly and run away. My heart is racing.

Nicole Smith (12)

**Maplewell Hall School, Loughborough**

# THE DAY I MET JLS

On Sunday I went to the shop to get a JLS CD. When I got to the shop I saw JLS signing books! They signed a photo for me and I was so happy. They sang a song especially for me and it was cool. They gave me a hug!

Stacey Stephens (12)

**Maplewell Hall School, Loughborough**

# THE ROBOT

A robot got into an aeroplane. It was the Prime Minister's plane. The robot took over the plane and crashed it. Everyone was dead.
The robot then took over the whole world and killed everyone. Then, when lots of time had passed, the robot crashed from cyber flu!

Kyale Cooper

**Maplewell Hall School, Loughborough**

# UNTITLED

The fairy godmother appeared with a beautiful long dress and glass slippers. She went to the ball and lost a slipper. Suddenly a prince came in and saw the glass slipper, he was searching for the owner but the ugly stepsisters got the slipper.

'Oh no, my slipper's gone!'

Amber Bourne (11)

**Monks' Dyke Technology College, Louth**

# THE BATTLE OF DEATH AND GLOOM

Gloom walked around the house. Death ran. Eliza roared inside ... the crying stopped. Her pounding heart did too. My crying started. Tears crowded out of my eyes. Gloom cheered with victory. Death did too. I dropped on the stone cold floor. Death had won. Death 2 - Gloom 1.

Kaydee Shepherd (11)

**Monks' Dyke Technology College, Louth**

# UNTITLED

Her name is Amy, she is beautiful and gifted. However, she has a problem. She is deaf. She only hears the sound of murder.
She obviously struggles at school but one gloomy day Amy hears a gunshot! Is it a friend or is it a complete stranger? Who knows ...?

Tom McGrath (11)

**Monks' Dyke Technology College, Louth**

# FISH VS MEGALODON VS SEAL

The fish raced to the rocks, knowing the seal would snap any second. The seal dodged falling ice.
'Finally,' said the fish.
He swam to the rocks when Megalodon struck.
'Phew!' said the fish.
The fish was blown out of the rocks. Megalodon had a little bonus. Poor fish.

Jake Havercroft (11)

**Monks' Dyke Technology College, Louth**

# HAMMER GUY

Around the corner there was a man with a hammer. He chased me all around the eerie town. Then the chase ended when there was a dead end. He had a big grin on his face, he was a scarface. He lifted his hammer and laughed ...

Nicholas Mountain (11)

**Monks' Dyke Technology College, Louth**

# UNTITLED

Suddenly I was being opened and then a big, fat, greasy hand, that smelt of pizza, dived into my foil, flimsy body and took one of my organs out. I heard a loud crunch and then a booming giant's voice, 'Want a Quaver?'

Violet Woods (11)

**Monks' Dyke Technology College, Louth**

# GHOST LAKE

The trees were rustling along the lake. The fisherman didn't know what was about to happen. The fisherman had caught something heavy, pulling the rod. The old man was dragged into the lake. He struggled and struggled. He shouted about in the remote river. No one ever saw him again.

Hannah Brocklebank (12)

**Monks' Dyke Technology College, Louth**

# TRAPPED ALIVE

*Snap!* went the wood as I walked across the uneven floorboards. Then *bang!* I fell to the ground. 'Ow!'
It was as black as midnight. I thought to myself *this can't be real! It's so damp down here, I hope someone comes and rescues me! If not I'm doomed!*

Chloe Bailey (12)

**Monks' Dyke Technology College, Louth**

# THE JUMP

She spun, leapt and turned. The competition had started. She came out into the middle of the ice. The music started; the tension began.

She was getting ready to jump when her mind went blank. She slowly fell to the ground, she tried to move but her legs wouldn't budge.

Amber Robinson (12)

**Monks' Dyke Technology College, Louth**

# THE TOYS

The toys in the workshop came alive at night. The twisted story tree started to unravel as it heard bells, talking and the till opening and closing.

Suddenly the shop door flew open and a figure darted to the open till and started unloading the cash into a bag.

Victoria Best (11)

**Monks' Dyke Technology College, Louth**

# THE CHASE

The stones crumbled as he ran to the edge of the cliff.
The small lion cub was being chased by zookeepers.
The poor little thing edged himself down to a ledge not
far down. He sat there for what seemed like hours, he
was saved.

Jasmine Snowden (11)

**Monks' Dyke Technology College, Louth**

# MY DEBUT

My heart was pounding when I strode onto the pitch.
It was one of my biggest games.
The game kicked off with one of my teammates darting
down the wing. The ball was crossed in but fell to my
feet, I skipped round the defender and shot ...

Euan Ross (11)

**Monks' Dyke Technology College, Louth**

# THE TORNADO

I ran as fast as my legs could carry me through the trees and bushes. The freak of nature followed me like a stalker. No matter where I ran it never went away! I climbed up a tree and shut my eyes tight. *This isn't real! What's going to happen?*

Charlotte Bray (11)

**Monks' Dyke Technology College, Louth**

# THE LIGHT

'Don't go in, it's too risky!' I desperately whimpered to him.
'But I have to find Mum!' Fred spoke with fear and discomfort.
Startled, I noticed a dazzling light from inside the cave. The blinding light forced me to look away. When the light vanished Fred had disappeared.

Sam Wattle (11)

**Monks' Dyke Technology College, Louth**

# ASSASSIN

I sprinted as fast as I could. I could hear him behind me. The drops of blood hitting the floor could be heard faintly. It was a dead end. I was dead.
He slashed his knife in front of me. It dug deeply into my forehead. I was dead!

Jack Winney (12)

**Monks' Dyke Technology College, Louth**

# PHEW!

I trembled with fear, sweat dripping from my T-shirt. The enormous spider looked as high as a house, with eyes like glowing dinner plates. It padded towards me quietly. *Crack!* The leaf on which I stood shivered, then slowly started breaking. I took a deep breath, dropping my magnifier. Phew!

Rachel Rolph (12)

**Monks' Dyke Technology College, Louth**

# THE SCARE

I crept across the dusty, musty floor. The huge abandoned house frightened me with its giant gaping windows. Unknown, four pairs of eyes stared at me from under a chair. Unblinking, unforgiving, the spider shot across the floor in front of me. I saw it. I screamed. Terrified, I ran.

Alice Rolph (12)

**Monks' Dyke Technology College, Louth**

# THE SHADOW

One dark, misty night a lady was walking home from the bingo when she saw a shadow dance across the wall. The lady sat in the bus shelter and felt the chilling cold against her face. The shadow started to shift towards her.
Suddenly the night was filled with a scream!

Siobhan Corcoran (12)

**Monks' Dyke Technology College, Louth**

# RUBY

My name is Ruby. Ruby red, a fiery colour like my life,
like my death. A stony heart and frozen blood.
I still feel the deadly teeth piercing my skin. Eyes red,
teeth sharp and the craving for blood. I will never forget
the day I became a vampire.

Elizabeth Nicholson (11)

**Monks' Dyke Technology College, Louth**

# UNTITLED

On Saturday morning I got up and went to the shop.
There I bought a lottery ticket for that night.
My wife said, 'It's a waste of money, you will not win.'
Later on I watched the lottery, then I knew I had won!

Joe Wrisdale

**Monks' Dyke Technology College, Louth**

# THE BLOWING

'There's a wind coming ... a strong wind,' I said to my friend.
'What do you mean?' she said.
'It's a strong wind and there is no way of surviving!'
I went into my bag and grabbed a mini fan and started laughing.
'Why did you do that?'
'Ha, ha!'

Rosie Jones (11)

**Monks' Dyke Technology College, Louth**

# HIGH UP IN THE TOWER

She was alone at the top of the castle, playing with her long, flowing hair. Her name was Rapunzel, she was a princess and she was waiting for a noble knight to come and rescue her from the dragon, Barasul.
'Zoe, stop playing with your toys. Now!'

Ryan Bingham (11)

**Monks' Dyke Technology College, Louth**

# THE FIGHTING BATTLE THAT MIGHT JUST GET YOU THINKING

She was alone, facing the biggest, scariest, bloodiest dragon she had ever seen. She fought with all her power, the mighty, blood-dripping beast was trying to win the battle with her …
'Okay, that's £3 please for the gingerbread.'
'Thank you!'

Hannah Sherrington (11)
**Monks' Dyke Technology College, Louth**

# THE THREE LITTLE BIRDS RAN AWAY

Once there were three birds. They decided to run away. Polly learnt to fly and moved in with Sally in the nest school, to learn too.
Once they had both learnt to build a nest and Polly to fly they went to live on their own with nests of their own.

Charlee McRae (12)
**Monks' Dyke Technology College, Louth**

# THE DEMON BARBER
# OF SCALP STREET

Screams came from Scalp Street. There was a demon disguised as a hairdresser. His next patient slouched and jumped into the chair.
'Now, just a trim?' the demon chuckled.
He sliced the innocent man's head in half and his brains sloshed onto the floor. His loud screams woke everyone up.

Oliver Ward (11)

**Monks' Dyke Technology College, Louth**

# RAMA AND SITA

Rama and Sita were banned from the kingdom for fourteen years. Life was hard at first.
While Rama was sent away his father passed away.
Sita was kidnapped by Ravenna, a demon of sorts.
Rama went to Luke for some help. There was a battle and Rama won.

Deanna Carden (11)

**Monks' Dyke Technology College, Louth**

# FIZZO THE MONKEY

Fizzo, the scratty monkey, was strolling along the beach. Fizzo was looking for sour bananas and suddenly he bumped into a beautiful monkey called Dilly, she had a fluffy orange flower placed on her ear.

They chatted all day and all night. They had things in common, perfect friends!

Leah Epton (11)

**Monks' Dyke Technology College, Louth**

# THE NIGHT TO REMEMBER

In the night of 6/12/2012 a girl was fast asleep having the worst dream; a dream about clowns and shadows, spinning round in her head and shadows in her room.

She woke. Phew! Just a dream. She turned over, clowns staring at her, she screamed very loudly.

Amy Favill (12)

**Monks' Dyke Technology College, Louth**

# DAUGHTER'S MOTHER DIED

Once upon a time lived a young girl. Her mother died when she was only a baby. She grew up with her father. When she was 18 her father died. Her new stepmother came along with her two daughters. She hated them and ran off.

Siobhan Hepworth (11)

**Monks' Dyke Technology College, Louth**

# UNTITLED

She was alone in the dark with no one to talk to. Blood dripping down the walls. She was terrified. She went downstairs, opened the door and she realised it was a nightmare.

Katie Williams (11)

**Monks' Dyke Technology College, Louth**

# UNTITLED

I was alone. I felt scared. I saw something go past me like a flash. I was scared that it was a ghost of my past. I looked around me, I saw nothing. But then I heard a big *bang!*
'Oh, it's just a dream. Goodnight.'

Courtney Ferguson (11)

**Monks' Dyke Technology College, Louth**

# VAMPIRES

Started at 9:30. There was an alarming tension in the atmosphere. I felt like I was being stalked. I spun around, I caught a glimpse of my night stalker. Lips trembling, I crept around the gloomy alley. My heart was thundering and there was a hovering vampire!
I was supper!

Ben Houlden (11)

**Monks' Dyke Technology College, Louth**

# ANGEL IN MY BASEMENT

Midnight; woke up by myself. The house was empty. My heart was trembling and thundering like a loud drum. I went to the kitchen, then down to the basement and saw a beloved angel. My eyes were shocked. It was a miracle. It was amazing, it was a dream!

Bradley Ogden (11)

**Monks' Dyke Technology College, Louth**

# UNTITLED

It was amazing, extraordinary. I looked around at the mysterious world before me. Snow was falling from the sky. I studied each flake of snow. They danced in the air, then formed a blanket of pure white on the ground.
Suddenly I heard footsteps behind me. Somebody else was there ...

Evie-Mae Lucas (11)

**Monks' Dyke Technology College, Louth**

# THE THING THAT WAKES ME UP

Every night I go to sleep in my old fashioned house. I get woken up by screaming and low-pitched thudding. I'm always scared to go out and find what the noise is, even if it's a dream. But this time I do ...
'I'm not alone in here!'

Darren Damms (12)
**Monks' Dyke Technology College, Louth**

# YOUR FINEST HOUR

June 6th 1944, D-Day. The waves of Northern France are lapping viciously up against the metallic coloured side of the landing craft.
'Go, go, go!' shouts a sergeant.
The terrified soldiers scramble out of the craft, bullets flying everywhere; but suddenly *boom!*
*Game over, please insert £1 to play again.*

George Duffield (12)
**Newbridge High School, Coalville**

# TIME'S UP

He poured the unusual powder into the container. Time was running out; he had to get the job done quickly. He calmly poured an amount of liquid into the container. The job was very nearly complete. There was just one more thing to do …
*Ping!*
'Holly, porridge is ready now!'

Lucy Saunders (12)
**Newbridge High School, Coalville**

# LITTLE RED RIDING HOOD

There I was, in the mist. The darkness of the gloomy forest …
A flash of grey appeared before me, a wolf! He stalled.
'You are …?' he growled as he turned human.
'L-L-Little Red Riding Hood.'
I started to run but he caught me! What would he do …?

Elliott Rees (11)
**Portland Comprehensive School, Worksop**

# ZOMBIE CITY

I dived through the window and heard a strange noise coming from upstairs. I got my shotgun out, I only had two bullets left but I continued up the stairs. I heard running, followed by roars. Before I knew it a zombie was charging at me.
I aimed at it ...

Oliver Booth (12)

**Portland Comprehensive School, Worksop**

# THE LOST DOG

There once was a lost and lonely dog who didn't have a home. Everyone thought he was a stray, so every time he went to a house they told him to go away.
But then, one day, he found a man and the man invited him in to stay.

Kathryn Harris (12)

**Portland Comprehensive School, Worksop**

# FALLING

We had just moved house in the middle of Worksop.
I decided to take the dog out. It wasn't dark but I was
still very cautious. I was just walking and the ground
gave way underneath my feet. I screamed.
I woke up ... Where was I? I was confused.

Jonathan Bailey (12)
**Portland Comprehensive School, Worksop**

# THE VISIT TO HELL

I was walking in the woods having a pleasant stroll.
*Crack!* Something huge was just behind me. I ran. The
ground fell away beneath me! I was falling down, past
fiery rocks and hard black stone.
I landed on my feet. Warm breath was pouring down
my neck ...
'Wake up!'

Amy Smith (11)
**Portland Comprehensive School, Worksop**

# WHAT WAS IT?

He walked to the graveyard to put some flowers on his grandad's grave. It was extremely late and the boy was very nervous.

All of a sudden, he could see that the graves had zombies coming out! They all went for the boy. He was terrified, he started screaming and ...

Robbie Manship (11)

**Portland Comprehensive School, Worksop**

# CHRISTMAS

*Bang!* I woke, it was Christmas Eve and I thought I'd heard someone. I heard it again. I went to wake my dad but he didn't believe me. *Bang!* There it was again. Dad went to see what it was. I looked out and Santa was lying on the ground ...

Charlotte Dilks (12)

**Portland Comprehensive School, Worksop**

# UNTITLED

He opened the door. I looked at his cruel wolf-like face.
'Trick or treat?' I said.
I saw a huge hand, it was like something from a horror movie. Suddenly I opened my eyes and rubbed them. It had all been a dream ... or was it?

Georgina Matthews (12)

**Portland Comprehensive School, Worksop**

# KING OF THE OCEAN

The freezing chill of the Alaskan Ocean waves hopped over the killer whale's tail as he looked out over the land for his next meal.
Killer whale, the king of the ocean, black as night, white eye and belly, was searching for his prey again.

Natalie Fisher (13)

**Portland Comprehensive School, Worksop**

# GHOSTLY BALLROOM

I was alone in the palace ballroom, just after the clock struck midnight. There was a dark, eerie feeling, then suddenly the tape player started spinning. 80s music started playing and my hips started moving. A cheery voice called out, 'Don't fight it! Feel it!'
I danced all night long.

Bethany Dobson (12)
**Portland Comprehensive School, Worksop**

# THE AFTERMATH

I stood frozen to the spot; terror paralysing me. I took in the horror in front of me. The mass of bloodied bodies, slowly drained of life, eyes forever open - staring at me.
I heard him walking to me, then I turned and looked at him …
'Why?'
'The aftermath!'

Rhiannon Ball (14)
**Portland Comprehensive School, Worksop**

# LITTLE RED RIDING HOOD

Hurriedly, she scurried through the dense forest. Panicking; she drove on, through the crawling ivy. She ran like her life depended on it, her dark hair flying back in the wind.
Suddenly she fell, her heart pounded. Getting up, she thought angrily, *I'll never get to Gran's on time!*

Elina Bennett (14)

**Portland Comprehensive School, Worksop**

# HOLIDAY ADVENTURES

I woke up in a strange tin room. This was not my room, the bed was uncomfortable and everything was creaking around me. Then I remembered ...
I hate caravan holidays!

Jordan Potter (12)

**Portland Comprehensive School, Worksop**

# MY AMAZING ADVENTURE

I went to Perth to see my dad and I saw a monstrous animal. It was there, at the end of the path and I was quaking in my boots; I did not know what to do. Then it leapt onto me, I screamed. 'Spider!'

Chloe Roe (12)

**Portland Comprehensive School, Worksop**

# THE HUNT

Its eyes glinted in the blinding sun, its heart raced. Its mouth watered with the thought of things to come ...
Then it caught its eye - fresh prey. Food! It tensed its muscles, ready to pounce. It let out a growl and darted forward. Outstretched limbs, finally satisfaction. The lion's hunt.

Hannah Sinnott (13)

**Portland Comprehensive School, Worksop**

# GHOST TRAIN

I looked around aimlessly into the darkness of the tunnel; strange noises screeched from high up in the old, rotten rafters. Something brushed against my cold face lightly and a harsh scream echoed around my head. Finally I rolled back into the open ...
The terror of a fairground ride.

Mhairi Macdonald (14)

**Portland Comprehensive School, Worksop**


# BEHIND YOU

*Bang!* The door closed. They turned. Ghostly figures were surrounding the room. They ran into the kitchen, the cooking utensils were floating. One more step they could have been dead.
Then the lights went off and the two kids were never heard nor seen again.

Danny Ashmore (13)

**Portland Comprehensive School, Worksop**

# VACANCY

I opened the window to our hotel room as I was hot.
I went to the bathroom after putting Amy to sleep. I
heard a scream, blinds flapping ... empty bed; trail of
blood!
I fell back against the wall, pale-faced, alone in a
foreign country, nobody but me. Alone.

Abbie Bartrop (14)
**Portland Comprehensive School, Worksop**

# THE BODY

*Bang!* The door slammed shut. His heart was throbbing,
his head spinning. The floor creaked ahead. He
wasn't alone. He noticed the blood first, bright red and
splattered all over the walls. He looked up, there was
the body, his spine sticking out. He turned, there was
the killer. Waiting ...

Thomas Askwith (14)
**Portland Comprehensive School, Worksop**

# JIMMY THE DREAMER

Jimmy dreamt about a girl all the time. But one night he knew it wasn't a dream! He sat up and stared hard at his empty room. Suddenly something dripped down his cheek! He looked up and saw the girl he had dreamt about. However, she was dead.

Georgie Brodie (13)

**Portland Comprehensive School, Worksop**

# SMOKE AND ASH

*Eeeek!* The door slowly creaks open. The two boys, Joe and Chris slowly creep in, followed by Carol holding onto Chris' hand, shivering in fright.

'Oooo!' A loud and sudden noise comes from the daunting cupboard, out flashes a disfigured figure, a sudden flash - nothing but smoke and ash.

Adam Wake (14)

**Portland Comprehensive School, Worksop**

# RUN

Shrinking back, the fog engulfing him, his friends were gone, tucked up in their beds. He was in the gloom, listening to the silence. The faint murmur in the distance struck him instantly.

'Danger! Run, run as fast as you can, I'm coming to eat you Gingerbread Man.'

Chloe Elwell (13)

**Portland Comprehensive School, Worksop**

# THE KNOCKING DOOR

The boy heard the knocking at the door for the fourth time. He was getting increasingly scared now. He had been alone in there for three hours. He was too scared and terrified to venture out from the room cast with shadows. The door flung open.

'Dinner's ready,' shouted Mum.

Emma Levitt (13)

**Portland Comprehensive School, Worksop**

# WHAT'S UNDER MY BED

It was dark. As soon as Molly's mum kissed her goodnight, it happened. Molly peered under her bed. She saw a small shadow, growing larger and larger. She looked up and saw a monster. She screamed and ran out. I just waited for her to switch the light on ...

Elizabeth Seyi (11)

**St Benedict Catholic School & Performing Arts College, Derby**

# THE CAT IN THE HAT

Just a normal day. Going fine till ... a knock on the door. That knock changed everything. It's the Cat in the Hat, there to annoy, bringing the thing things with him. My brother is allergic to cats so I buy a dog. *Bark!* 'Argh!' And that's how you lose a cat.

Amanda Hoyte-Morris (12)

**St Benedict Catholic School & Performing Arts College, Derby**

# WHAT IT'S LIKE WHEN YOU FALL IN LOVE

The day was beautiful. I went for a run. I was in the park when I instantly fell in love. Our eyes met and we froze right there, it was magical! We stood there just looking at each other. That was when I realised he was the one!

Holly Analise Hadley (11)

**St Benedict Catholic School & Performing Arts College, Derby**

# THE DAY MY HAMSTER DIED

I woke up and walked downstairs. My sister came up with my hamster and said, 'He's gone Imie.'
I said, 'What do you mean?'
She said, 'He's dead.' I started crying my eyes out; My mum kept me off. Me and Jacob buried him that night. I still miss him.

Imogen Hayward (12)

**St Benedict Catholic School & Performing Arts College, Derby**

# MERLIN AND THE KILLERS!

'Quick Merlin, they're coming, get my men ready ... we are going to kill them all.'
'Arthur, how are you going to? They have used magic, they will live forever. If you kill them they will come back to life!'
'Merlin, listen to me ... go and get my men ready *now!*'

Shannon Edwards (11)

**St Benedict Catholic School & Performing Arts College, Derby**

# THE CHEESE

'Could I have the pasta with ... some extra cheese?' asked the man on table three.
'Yes,' replied the waiter.
The man twiddled his thumbs. Five minutes had passed. The waiter brought the food. He placed it on the table and walked away. 'No!' screamed the man, 'where's my extra cheese?'

Rachel Herbert (11)

**St Benedict Catholic School & Performing Arts College, Derby**

# LITTLE JUMPING GRANNY

Her mum told Red Riding Hood to visit her gran and give her cakes. She was happily jumping in the woods when a wolf said, 'Can I come to Gran's?'
She replied, 'Of course you can.'
When they got there Gran shouted, 'Howling noises are coming from the window!'

Malisha Stanley (12)

**St Benedict Catholic School & Performing Arts College, Derby**

# THE TINY BUT BRAVE

Once upon a time, there was a tiny cottage and in that cottage there were tiny people. One day the tiny people who were called Fred, Mike and Bob were attacked by a tiny lion. The tiny lion roared, 'I want a biscuit!'
Fred replied, 'Alright, but say please.'

Seanna McGirr (12)

**St Benedict Catholic School & Performing Arts College, Derby**

# MY GOLDFISH IS EVIL

One stormy day my goldfish was working out how to keep the weather bad forever! He turned the power to max on his dodgy-looking machine. A sign started to flash saying: *Power Overload.* Steam burst out of the vent! *Warning: Power Overload! Splat!* He'd put the piesplat in instead!

Joseph Clark (11)

**St Benedict Catholic School & Performing Arts College, Derby**

# NOW YOU KNOW WHY ROSIE HATES GHOSTS!

Rosie felt a cold wind wake her from her sleep. She knew what was there. A ghost, called Dispare. He howled and booed, destroying her room. 'Dispare!' she screeched, 'Go away!'
'Rosie,' he growled, 'is the chippy open?'
'No! get a life!'
'Can't. I'm a ghost!' he laughed, howling madly.

Lucy Regan (11)

**St Benedict Catholic School & Performing Arts College, Derby**

# THE GOK WAN WOLF

Rachel was strolling through the woods when she could see a pair of fixed yellow eyes watching her every move. She was terrified. Her palms were sweaty, her dress was sticking to her back. She thought this was the end. When suddenly a wolf jumped out and exclaimed, 'Hey girlfriend!'

Corah Gritton (11)

**St Benedict Catholic School & Performing Arts College, Derby**

# THE BUTTERFLY LION

I've done it, away from the horrifying screams. Constant bullying, the wicked slap of the powerful cane across my sweaty palms. I climb nervously up the wobbly fence. Somebody spots me. I sprint as fast as a lion, but too late, an old lady running towards me breathlessly, 'Hey you!'

Thomas Payne (11)

**St Benedict Catholic School & Performing Arts College, Derby**

# TAKEN

A couple had moved into a house. On their first night there they heard footsteps. Nobody was there. But one night they were both awake. They looked at the bottom of their bed and something looked at them. They ran into the corner and they haven't been seen since.

Joel Callaghan (11)

**St Benedict Catholic School & Performing Arts College, Derby**

# 13

It was a normal day for Yakamoshi and Dave. They lived in a mansion two miles wide and three miles upwards! There were 13 rooms in the colossal building.

One day Yakamoshi was at Morrisons; Dave decided to go up to the 13th room ... *Boom!* He was gone straight away ...

Luke Bromage (12)

**St Benedict Catholic School & Performing Arts College, Derby**

# FRIGHTENED

A young boy called James was walking home and saw a little boy was getting beaten up in the street outside his house. He didn't know what to do; he ran around the back of his house thinking, *what shall I do?* So he ran through the back door! 'Dad!'

Monty Rai (12)

**St Benedict Catholic School & Performing Arts College, Derby**

# THE DARK STAIRS

Lisa dithered on the stairs, walking up tentatively in the darkness. There was a bright light and booming loud voices at the top. Lisa wondered curiously, *has it started?* As she edged to the top step, she stared in disbelief. She was late. The movie had already begun.

Dakshayeeni Sivasankaran (12)

**St Benedict Catholic School & Performing Arts College, Derby**

# THE BEAST OF THE DARK

I opened my eyes, I could feel its breath blowing my hair off. The dark figure jumped out of the wilderness and landed with a thud, shaking the ground as it landed, blowing the rotting leaves into the distance. The beast's eyes were deep sapphire, glaring at me with confusion.

Matthew Connolly (12)

**St Benedict Catholic School & Performing Arts College, Derby**

# THE SUBWAY TRAIN

We sat in a small, congested space. We zoomed into the endless darkness. A dull light flickered above our heads. People's faces were grim and lifeless. They breathed heavily. There was no life outside. Then the windows lit up. An emotionless voice came from above. 'All stops for Piccadilly Circus!'

Lily Moss (12)

**St Benedict Catholic School & Performing Arts College, Derby**

# CREEPY DARKNESS

I'd opened my eyes, everything was dark. I thought, *it's night,* but suddenly, I saw a bright light and a creepy sound coming from my right side. I was frightened to death. I ran forward and cried. It was scary and creepy in there, but I knew that I'd escape.

Patryk Wypasek (13)

**St Benedict Catholic School & Performing Arts College, Derby**

# WHAT IS THAT?

I was woken up by the sound of a horrible voice calling my name. I opened my eyes to see what it was. It had big ears, beady eyes, and a big nose. 'Wake up, you're going to be late for school!' It was my mum!
'Do I have to?'

Kane Williamson (12)

**St Benedict Catholic School & Performing Arts College, Derby**

# NO TURNING BACK

I wanted to get out but I couldn't, it had such a tight grip on me. The look on people's faces made me even more scared. They screamed uncontrollably; some even cried! I thought it would never end. I tried to cover my eyes. 'The roller coaster is now over.'

Jada Williamson (12)

**St Benedict Catholic School & Performing Arts College, Derby**

# A JOURNEY WITH A TWIST AND TURN

I woke up on a sunny Sunday morning to find darkness all around me. I was petrified to see a beam of yellow light carrying me up in mid-air onto this spaceship. There were aliens around me. I saw a beam of light. I ran for my little life …

Ryan Moon (12)

**St Benedict Catholic School & Performing Arts College, Derby**

# THE BIG DOOR

I walked down the dark street, slowly I crept towards the big open door. Should I go in? I did anyway. I reluctantly stepped up the step and walked into the main hall. It was covered with cobwebs and dust. It was also very cold. I heard a sharp noise ...

Iesha Doman (13)

**St Benedict Catholic School & Performing Arts College, Derby**

# CREEPY GRAVEYARD DREAM

I was walking through the graveyard then I looked behind me. A zombie was following me. I ran, then I tripped. I saw a haunted house, went towards it. The door crept open ... then I woke up sweating. I got out of bed.

Tiffany Rice (12)

**St Benedict Catholic School & Performing Arts College, Derby**

# CRUSH OF FEAR

As the sharp and fierce knife cut through, I could smell the power whipping the poor thing. The tension was building up, bit by bit. The thing was dripping endlessly, smelling it was killing me slowly. Tall, bald man, his hands stained with blood. 'Thanks for cutting the steak.'

Kayvan Karimi (12)

**St Benedict Catholic School & Performing Arts College, Derby**

# HOME ALONE ...
# IN DARKNESS

'Twas 1831. John lay awake on his bed. He was home alone until Dad got back at 12:30. Fighting the dark, John reached for his matches when suddenly they were placed in his hands. 'Here you go son!' a voice muttered as the lights came on. John's clock chimed ... 12:30!

Kallum Bracken (12)

**St Benedict Catholic School & Performing Arts College, Derby**

# THE SCARY CELLAR

The lights flickered in the air. Then suddenly a light blew up, blinding me for a few seconds. I was walking down into the dark, damp cellar then a dog appeared. It started to chase me. I realised then it was only the ghost of the woman who'd died there.

Ellis Butcher (10)

**St Benedict Catholic School & Performing Arts College, Derby**

# THE GREATEST MOMENT

He struck the ball at full power; it seemed nothing could stop it. It was destined for the top corner. It would win his team the final. It hit the back of the net, he celebrated enthusiastically. 'Nothing gets better than that feeling!' the player later exclaimed!

Joe Condon (13)

**St Benedict Catholic School & Performing Arts College, Derby**

# DEAD END

The killer approached, his beady eyes darted everywhere, making sure there were no witnesses. His eyes flickered back to me, cold and gleaming with satisfaction. I scuffled backwards, *Thud!* A dead end. I looked around helplessly. Nothing. All I could do was watch as he approached ... 'Tag! You're it!'

Dessa Mariah Agcaoili (13)

**St Benedict Catholic School & Performing Arts College, Derby**

# THE SIGHTING

The old door creaked open. Spiderwebs draped down from the dusty ceiling. 'Hello?' Silence, except for a ghostly voice echoing in the distance. I tiptoed upstairs and into a little room, only to find strange-looking shadows hanging from the ceiling. I switched on the light. I stared in horror ...

Chloe Detheridge (13)

**St Benedict Catholic School & Performing Arts College, Derby**

# THE SHADOW

It was a dark night. The lights were off. A shadow appeared from nowhere. 'It's a ghost,' said Lucy. The shadow came towards the girls. 'Argh!'
The light turned on. 'Oh Dad!'

Farai Wasarirevu (12)

**St Benedict Catholic School & Performing Arts College, Derby**

# MY MIDNIGHT HORROR

All I had was a mean stepmother, two horrible sisters, basically a sad life! They locked me in a gloomy, dark room. For at least a week I was locked in this room with only three glasses of water! 'Oh, a switch.' *Flick.* I was in my bedroom!

Weronika Hardy (12)

**St Benedict Catholic School & Performing Arts College, Derby**

# THE DEAD

It was a dark night like every other, but somehow it was different. It just felt weird. Then, in the distance, I saw a shadow. It did not look like a human. It looked like a dead man! It got closer and closer. Then I remembered - it was Halloween!

Freddie Elliott (12)

**St Benedict Catholic School & Performing Arts College, Derby**

# UNTITLED

Cinderella is born, abandoned, slave of her evil stepmother and ugly stepsisters. Her fairy godmother magically makes her a dress for the ball. She meets Prince Charming, but then Cinderella runs away, Prince Charming searches everywhere, finds her, and they live happily ever after.

Lauren Hannah (12)

**St Benedict Catholic School & Performing Arts College, Derby**

# LIL GREEN ALIENS

Ethan, the smallest alien on Planet Depar, went to the Special Academy for Green Aliens. Ethan was bullied by the taller aliens because of his size. So one day he built a machine that made him two times larger. He then went on to become Ethan, Protector of Depar.

Parrish Gayle (12)

**St Benedict Catholic School & Performing Arts College, Derby**

# THE DARK NIGHT

A dark night stood between him and his house. He started crossing the dark gloomy road. His heart was racing as he moved his foot onto the road. *Thud.* He heard his foot hit the road. Everything suddenly slowed down as he looked around him.

Emily Randle (12)

**St Benedict Catholic School & Performing Arts College, Derby**

# HAPPY BIRTHDAY

One day a man went to a club at about 8pm with his son who felt excited and ecstatic about going to the club. The anxious father felt very strange and his blood went cold. When he got there he saw darkness. The light came on. People said, 'Happy birthday!'

James Coleman (12)

**St Benedict Catholic School & Performing Arts College, Derby**

# THE THING

The thing towered over me, I could smell its hot, misty breath, hear it panting. It was about to strike. Its long, sharp claws came down, like a lightning bolt. Suddenly, I heard a bang, the creature toppled over, howling in pain. A figure emerged from the mist. The farmer!

Joseph Daubney (13)

**St Benedict Catholic School & Performing Arts College, Derby**

# THE LOST WAND

One day a fairy lost her wand. She didn't know what to do. She looked everywhere. She even looked under her toaster. But then she remembered, she'd put it under her pillow. She flew upstairs and to her bedroom, and she found it. What a relief.

Angela Namkumba (12)

**St Benedict Catholic School & Performing Arts College, Derby**

# THE JAWS OF THE SEA

As I looked behind me I could see the jaws of the beast, getting closer and closer to the boat. I jumped to the front, as its jaws crushed the boat bit by bit. Suddenly the boat stuttered and I fell into the water. I was sure I would die!

William Monange (12)

**St Benedict Catholic School & Performing Arts College, Derby**

# THE VAMPIRE QUEEN

Severus grabbed Alisha by her wrist. Alisha screamed for him to let her go and he said no. Meanwhile Isabella found her mother's wand. As Isabella gave the wand to Mother, Severus never spoke again about Alisha. Alisha was the vampire queen and her family were never ever underestimated again.

Alisha Hales (13)

**St Benedict Catholic School & Performing Arts College, Derby**

# UNTITLED

It was Christmas Day and a young girl called Shannon wished for the perfect Christmas Day. Later that day she got everything she wanted; a lovely pink dress and a pair of sparkly red shoes. The Christmas dinner was delicious. Yummy, turkey and stuffing. It was the best day ever.

Shannon Vallely (12)

**St Benedict Catholic School & Performing Arts College, Derby**

# THE DRAGON TAMER AND THE GOLDEN DRAGON

In my time, there are dragons; my dream is to become a dragon tamer. To ride one of the beasts, soaring through the sky. Too bad that won't happen, I have completed almost every test. I need to capture an uncaptured dragon. The golden dragon. So the adventure starts here!

Ryan Molloy (12)

**St Benedict Catholic School & Performing Arts College, Derby**

# THE UNEXPECTING ARCHAEOLOGIST

Walking through the forest the archaeologist found a tomb so he went to explore ... When he got in he saw gold and lots of it. But then he walked closer. He heard a click. He was trapped. It was too late. An arrow came. He died.

Darragh Ashley (12)

**St Benedict Catholic School & Performing Arts College, Derby**

# GLISTENED

On a cold winter's night, the snow glistened on the web. Right in the middle of the web was a spider. Starved, as no bugs were around because of the frost until ... *Ping!* The spider spun around the lifeless moth. Satisfied, it crawled away. The moonlight sparkled on the web.

Molly Jennings (12)

**St Benedict Catholic School & Performing Arts College, Derby**

# THE FROZEN TOILET AT GRANDAD'S

Harold was my grandad: a man of intelligence. He fought through wars and had an 18th century house. He had problems when he grew old and trouble with his electricity, he'd put it in himself. His house, over time, had rotted away, he even had a frozen toilet in winter.

Charles Gamblin (11)

**St Benedict Catholic School & Performing Arts College, Derby**

# THE TOUCH OF A BAUBLE

'Yay!' I shrieked as I put my favourite bauble on the glistening Christmas tree; it gave me a gentle shiver as I touched it with the tip of my finger to be transported to Glaciar! This land looks the same as in the bauble: Magical! I cannot believe it!

Abbie Sharpe (12)

**St Benedict Catholic School & Performing Arts College, Derby**

# THE SMELL OF SMOKE

Jane awoke to the smell of smoke. She went to her window to look. Pudding Lane was on fire. 'Get up Jane. We have to leave on our boat, take everything you need,' shouted Mother. Jane got ready, then ran to her boat. She was safe, but people were suffering.

Eloise Hadson (12)

**St Benedict Catholic School & Performing Arts College, Derby**

# THE INVENTION THAT NEVER HAPPENED

It was a gloomy night when I completed my invention. I started it up and *bang!* I stood in shock. What had happened? Did I do something wrong? I grabbed my box of most precious possessions and flew out the door. I watched my house burn down. I had survived!

Charlotte Warren (11)

**St Benedict Catholic School & Performing Arts College, Derby**

# THE MONSTER INVASION

I was terrified. They were coming closer. What was going to happen? Were they good or evil? Should I run or stay? What were they? They had brown eyes and brown bodies with a big curly tail. 'They're only monkeys darling,' whispered Mum, comforting me instantly.

Owen Butler (11)

**St Benedict Catholic School & Performing Arts College, Derby**

# UNTITLED

White surrounding me. Silky snow under my feet. I can't see anything beyond me. Snowflakes on my eyelashes. Kids hurling snowballs at each other. People making snowmen. It is a freezing day, everyone is wrapped up warm. On my way to school. Why is it so cold?

Jessica Plant (11)

**St Benedict Catholic School & Performing Arts College, Derby**

# DRESS SHOPPING GONE WRONG

New York City, a city made up of shops. Dresses, shoes, handbags, head rags, anything you can imagine! But if you let a friend pick a bridesmaid's dress out, you'll end up looking like a sea turtle! If only I'd tried to change her mind. New York had other plans …

Harriet Russ (11)

**St Benedict Catholic School & Performing Arts College, Derby**

# KITTENS JUST LIKE MINE

One beautiful summer's day, I watched my kitten chasing a butterfly. She chased it up the garden and up the tree. She disappeared, I was worried. I started crying, Sheba was gone.

Later, Sheba wandered back wet, dribbling and feeling sorry for herself. I started drying and cleaning her up.

Sophie Jane Churchill (11)

**St Benedict Catholic School & Performing Arts College, Derby**

# THE NATURE MONSTER

One dark night three boys decided to explore the forbidden woods. They soon got lost and sat under a tree.

The next morning the tree wasn't there, all they could see were giant footprints. They heard a low growl behind them. They didn't survive another five seconds.

Piotr Klukowicz (11)

**St Benedict Catholic School & Performing Arts College, Derby**

# THE SUN

The night was over and the dawn had broken. A fireball shot up in the sky. The night was perishing but now as a ray of light shone down on me, I felt the warmth and an unusual shiver went down my spine. The sun had risen once more.

Chinju George (12)

**St Benedict Catholic School & Performing Arts College, Derby**

# ONE DARK NIGHT

Once there was a boy called Tom. He had a brother called Jim who made Tom angry. One dark night when everything was quiet Tom crept into Jim's room with an axe and crept back out.
The next day Tom's mother woke up Tom, to tell him Jim was dead.

Merlin Joy (11)

**St Benedict Catholic School & Performing Arts College, Derby**

# CITY'S DOOM

Disease had spread to the village. Two men could save us. One man could go. I was one of those men but I was not the chosen one, I'm a wizard. I tried to help him, he refused. Now the village is doomed until a new hero comes to light.

Charlie Young (11)

**St Benedict Catholic School & Performing Arts College, Derby**

# UNTITLED

'Where am I?' Bob turned the TV on to see … instead of the news, a game flashed before his eyes.
'You need to find a key,' the TV said. 'It is hidden in your bedroom.'
'I see it!' He broke the telly and the key was there. Phew!

Ben Morley (11)

**St Benedict Catholic School & Performing Arts College, Derby**

# WHAT TO CALL MY SURPRISE

In the car, 'Where am I going? That noise … is it … Puppies!' So small, so fluffy! My favourite chocolate Labrador. I saw him jumping and barking, so cute, with big paws. 'I want him, but what to call him? I think Gus. It's something new, it's something cute!'

Lucy Barber (13)

**St Benedict Catholic School & Performing Arts College, Derby**

# THE LAST GORGON

I trembled vigorously, bathing in my own sweat. One glance was all it took, but my eyes were hypnotised by the beauty. The beauty of the creature, with writhing serpents for hair. She rose up from the icy azure depths as I felt my flesh turn to stone. *Game Over!*

Madona George (14)

**St Benedict Catholic School & Performing Arts College, Derby**

# THE CHOCOLATE SHOP

I strolled to the shop. I saw lotsa chocolate, I like chocolate. I whipped the £50 note out of my pocket and gave it to the shopkeeper. 'Give me all your chocolate!' I declared.
My Mum is now angry with me because I didn't get milk. And now I'm fat.

Oliver Turner (13)

**St Benedict Catholic School & Performing Arts College, Derby**


# THE OUTSIDE

As I strolled down the hollow woods, following trolls and pixies all with goods, I know I don't belong here. I've got nothing to say. I'm only going to be here till the end of the day. Mysteries and secrets all revealed. Kept from outsiders with a shield ... Busted.

Naydine Mason (13)

**St Benedict Catholic School & Performing Arts College, Derby**

# NO EMERGENCY

The princess skipped towards her palace. She noticed the window was smashed. Her face dropped. She ran towards the broken glass. She peered through. Her unicorn was watching TV. The princess realised that it had jumped through the window and there was no emergency.

Hope Piercy (14)

**St Benedict Catholic School & Performing Arts College, Derby**

# ARACHNOPHOBIA

I sit cowering in the corner. The shadow on the wall is an emphasis of my fear. Crawling, scrawny, eight-legged thing, beady eyes watching me closely. My heart is racing, I can feel it drumming in my ears. Closer, closer it comes up to me, I'm struck still, frozen.

Charlotte Warden (14)

**St Benedict Catholic School & Performing Arts College, Derby**

# FRIDAY THE 13TH

It is a dark, rainy night. Some teenagers arrive at a camp. They build a fire, set up their tents, get their chairs out ... There is a murderer on the loose. He hides away into the night, to kill the teenagers. It is Friday the 13th.

Declan Smith (13)

**St Benedict Catholic School & Performing Arts College, Derby**

# IGNORED

It was an ordinary day for an ordinary girl. She was trying to get some attention from the teachers but they were ignoring her.

Sometimes she's lazy, she gets bored, but anything could happen in this world for an ordinary girl. She had no friends, alone, poor little girl.

Sandra Gudidis (13)

**St Benedict Catholic School & Performing Arts College, Derby**

# UNTITLED

A prince rode down a long, winding, cobbly path. He stumbled across a tiny red mushroom. He then picked it up. The horse mistook it for food and munched on it. He then turned ginger and trotted away. The prince stared in wonder and awe, then he struggled home.

Zea Therese Smith (13)

**St Benedict Catholic School & Performing Arts College, Derby**

# ARE YOU COMING OR WHAT?

On a cold, frosty, winter's night, I looked aimlessly at the humungous magnificent building in front of me. My true love would peer out of the window and throw down her long, beautiful blonde hair. I waited, no answer. I waited … I would have to do this the hard way …

Matthew Szczomak (14)

**St Benedict Catholic School & Performing Arts College, Derby**

# RAPUNZEL - THE UNTOLD STORY

She let her hair drape down the magnificent tower. 'Climb up!' she shouted. The prince, unsure, carefully placed one hand on the lengthy plait, prepared himself to jump and then tugged hard, trying to hoist himself up. All of a sudden the plait came falling down the tower. Extensions!

Ellie Nicholas (13)

**St Benedict Catholic School & Performing Arts College, Derby**

# UNTITLED

She was beautiful. Everything I'd ever dreamed. Lovely, blonde hair, gorgeous blue eyes - she reminded me of 'Cinderella', perfect in every way, she was walking towards me, what to do? Stand there? Run away? 'We should meet up sometime.' The glisten in her eye said my dreams had come true.

Alexandra Worthington (14)

**St Benedict Catholic School & Performing Arts College, Derby**

# THE STRANGER

He stands there with a sinister look on his old guilty face. I can only hear his footsteps and the tears of others. He reaches his hand into his pocket and ... says, 'Can you finish your maths work please?'

Ben Bushnell (14)

**St Benedict Catholic School & Performing Arts College, Derby**

# THE FIGHT FOR SURVIVAL

I lose. I fall. I win. I stay standing. I fall again. I'm fighting a losing battle. A hunk eats my soul for his survival. I give up. I can't go on any longer. I'm defeated by the hunk named Devil. I die for the Earth's survival.

Gemma Amos (12)

**Spalding High School, Spalding**

# MY WONDERFUL FURRY BOOTS

When I got my furry boots I was very proud. Proud of my silky, comfortable boots. I wore them every day. But then came the dreaded day ... I lost my furry boots! I was so upset and down but then I realised, they were under my bed the whole time.

Emily Christina Viller (12)

**Spalding High School, Spalding**

# THE OPERATION

Sweat was dripping off my forehead. I had very wobbly hands. Blood was everywhere. I was now in charge of his life. His heart was pounding in front of my eyes. I could hear the heart monitor getting slower every minute. His heart stopped beating, but he was blinking.

Chloe Fisher (11)

**Spalding High School, Spalding**

# OH HAPPY DAYS!

I stopped. There he was, waiting at the corner. The cutest boy in the whole school was staring at *me!* His eyes twinkled, he flicked his fringe and grinned a large, glistening grin. I looked behind and there was his girlfriend, waving at him. He waved back. Lord help me!

Francesca Hayward (11)
**Spalding High School, Spalding**

# A GHOST'S LAMENT

I remember getting my first car. I remember the first time I met my wife. I remember the day my daughter was born. I remember getting snow on Christmas Day. I remember my fortieth birthday but I can't remember how I died.

Heather Montgomery (13)
**Spalding High School, Spalding**

# HIS GAZE

I was glaring at my science exercise book; it made no sense to me to be completely honest. The boy sitting next to me looked at me questioningly. I lifted up my head to meet his gaze. It was like a fairy tale, lost in the moment. Never looking back.

Penelope Gladwin (13)

**Spalding High School, Spalding**

# THE PTERODACTYL

The mother pterodactyl was sleeping. I could hear the egg cracking. Soon the egg would crack! All of a sudden the mother pterodactyl screamed and I covered my ears and closed my eyes. When I opened my eyes I saw my mother holding my new little baby brother. Hooray!

Annabelle Lane (12)

**Spalding High School, Spalding**

# BULLET

I can feel their icy gaze on my back. I turn around, I see the trigger ... the bullet, time is slowing. I move, but not quick enough. My arm ... They are coming. I can see their emotionless, unforgiving expressions. My eyesight's fading ... My breaths are growing shorter ... I'm dying.

Morgan Agate (12)

**Spalding High School, Spalding**

# THE MAN WHO HAD A DREAM!

There was a beautiful young man who walked through the forest. He was called Matt. One day he met a delightful young girl in the forest. Matt proposed to her and she agreed with such enjoyment. They had a very happy life and then they lived happily ever after. Hooray!

Rhiannon Hardman (12)

**Spalding High School, Spalding**

# PRINCE EDWARD

After years of searching, Prince Edward reached a town with a beautiful palace. Edward galloped to the magical palace. A truly beautiful princess appeared, wearing a magnificent dress. It was love at first sight. The princess had to let him down gently. She had married her prince charming last year.

Jordan Pope (11)

**Spalding High School, Spalding**

# FLYING, IS IT POSSIBLE?

He was flying, he didn't know how but just knew he was. He was in the sky one minute but not the next. He was falling to the earth at the speed of light. 'Someone help!' he shouted, no one knew how though. He looked terrified, shaking in his boots!

Lucy Marshall (11)

**Spalding High School, Spalding**

# HE'S COMING!

Quick, run to my bed before he comes! I really hope he's got me what I've always wanted. I hear sleigh bells ringing. I shut my eyes and try to dream. I hear, 'Ho! Ho!' Then a *crash! Bang! Wallop!* Then sudden silence.
I wake Mum and Dad. 'Run, now!'

Katie Hurst (11)

**Spalding High School, Spalding**

# GUNPOINT

I step forward, gun on my neck. Sweat dripping, scared of the unknown. My wedding ring burns my heart. Tears prickle in my eyes as the police arrive. Everything is a blur.
*Bang! Boom!* I hear shots, then it fades, it all fades. I have an hour left.

Emily Ormes (11)

**Spalding High School, Spalding**

# WILL ANYBODY MISS ME?

I'd had an argument. I went to the corner shop, smoked my last cigarette. Walked to all the places I might miss. If dead people can miss. I stepped onto the bridge. Hung a rope around my neck. Will anybody miss me? Guess I will never find out.

Sophie Ashdown (11)

**Spalding High School, Spalding**

# NIGHT OF THE LIVING DOLL

'What's that?' Jaden said as he and William heard a squeak.
'Don't know,' William cried. The squeak got closer and closer until it revealed a doll.
'Oh,' they said. The doll moved her legs as the doctor entered the room. The doll attacked the doctor. As she did they ran.

Georgina Jagger (11)

**Sutherland House School, Nottingham**

# THE SNOW MONSTER

It snowed heavily. I made a snowman. I called him Fred. He told me he would eat me. I tried to destroy him. He tried to destroy me. I told my mum but she didn't believe me. Fred ate me.
He is a monster and I am a scary ghost.

Aoife Rhodes (13)

**The Becket School, Wilford**

# I'M COMING TO GET YOU

*Thump!* I sat up in my bed. 'Mum? Dad?' I called. I was getting really scared. 'Mum? Dad?'
Then a voice, 'I've got your mum. I'm coming to get you. I've got your dad. I'm coming to get you. I've got your sisters. I'm coming to get you.'
*Thump!* 'Argh!'

James Moore (12)

**The Becket School, Wilford**

# THE DIVE

It swooped through the air, focusing on the object, penetrating the sky as it dived. It twisted and turned elegantly as it curved back up to the skyline. It magnificently flew towards the sunset, beating its wings strongly. Blood dripping from its prey as he ripped angrily at the limbs.

Daniel Vipond (11)

**The Becket School, Wilford**

# GUESS THE RULES

Lies could break it. Over controlling you is the way it works. Very powerful, it has no limit. Everyone needs this in their life because it's so important.
Look at the first letter of each sentence ... It spells love.
These are rules of love.

Hazel Hurboda (11)

**The Becket School, Wilford**

# THE ADVENTURES OF JAMES SNOTTER

James was facing the evil Moldymort, it was war.
Moldymort waved his wand and said, 'Boildormash.'
James jumped out the way. 'You want kill me
Moldymort,' and then, 'exspelliamus!'
Shocked, the potato man said, 'What are you on about?
I said potato or mash?'
'Oh, I'll have mash please sir.'

Sebastian Channell (11)

**The Becket School, Wilford**

# SOMETHING HEARTBREAKING

Something heartbreaking has happened. I'm on my
own and I'm determined to take care of myself but
facing the truth is hard. With help and love from my
grandmother and letters I write, can I start to see all is
not lost and I can get my life back?

Chloe Carpenter (12)

**The Becket School, Wilford**

# WHAT IF ...?

What if ...? What if the flowing water rivers turned into a dark gloopy chocolate? What if the day after Saturday was Wednesday? What if the luxurious grass of the meadows turned blue? What if we could fly? What would the world be like? In one boy's world this really happened!

Olivia Griffiths (12)

**The Becket School, Wilford**

# THE HOTEL HAUNT

One dark and stormy night three men sat in a hotel. The lights began to flicker, the picture started to sway. They ran towards the door, but it slammed shut! Suddenly a figure stood in the doorway and exclaimed, 'You might think this is over but the game's just begun!'

Paigane-Jayne Hallam Bennett (12)

**The Becket School, Wilford**

# THE TERROR

There was terror in their faces. They ran away. From what? I didn't know. I couldn't see. There was a shriek. I stopped - I saw what they were running from. There was a cold hand on my shoulder that sent shivers down my spine. This was the day I died.

Kathleen Blake (13)

**The Becket School, Wilford**

# IS THIS THE END?

There I was, frozen still as a rock. Was it now that my life was going to end? All my memories flashed before my eyes as the bright light came closer. The honk of a car bellowed but I could not move. My heart raced faster than ever before …

Amber Williams (13)

**The Becket School, Wilford**

# A BLUE BLANKET

The stormy sea crashed heavily against the damp rocks as I gazed longingly out to the horizon. A tap on the back woke me from my awe and wonder. I turned to find an old man, with such stories from the past of the blue blanket before my eyes.

Jasmin Pacey-Devlin (12)

**The Becket School, Wilford**

# PARALYSED BY DEATH

I lay there, on the ice-cold pavement. Paralysed, not being able to move. In a daze. I could still feel the knife in my back. Now feelings were coming back to me: the metallic taste of blood. But suddenly death punched me in the face. Darkness engulfed me ...

Stephen Ramsden (13)

**The Becket School, Wilford**

# HORROR IN THE HAUNTED HOUSE!

The floors were creaking, the bats were squeaking, the children were scared. Back home their parents were biting their nails with worry. There was a sudden gunshot from the haunted house. The mum fainted and the dad screamed, then there was an ambulance siren. All was carefully explaining after.

Isabelle Uren (13)

**The Becket School, Wilford**

# THE MATCH

Currie FC against Lombaster United is surely going to be a cracking game but there's someone running on the field. He has just stuck something in the ground and the ground is opening up. Everyone is getting sucked into the ground but there is someone on the roof. Brilliant goal.

Jack Maguire-Thompson (11)

**The Becket School, Wilford**

# THE DISTANT NEBULA

They passed the crimson red nebula when the ship was struck by a meteor. Skilfully John, the captain of the ship, weaved in and out of the asteroid belt. They passed the giant planet, Jupiter. They encountered a black hole. They controlled it to safety and made it to Earth.

Matthew Currie (12)

**The Becket School, Wilford**

# A LITTLE BIT OF MAGIC

Once upon a time the knights of the Round Table went to war. They fought against the wizard Zalock. Many men were lost in the battles. Eventually one knight reached Zalock's lair. He clenched his sword and cut through his chest. Peace was returned in the valley. Until next time.

Ellie Courtney (13)

**The Becket School, Wilford**

# CHIPS

Axel knew a man who made drum kits. One day Axel went to ask for a drum kit. He banged hard on the door. The man answered in a gruff voice, 'Who is it?'
'It's me, Axel.' Slowly he answered the door, mouth dripping with red liquid.
'Fancy some chips?'

James Shepherd (12)
**The Becket School, Wilford**

# WELL?

She knew it was her turn now. Her friends had done it. But those hawk-like eyes were staring at her, seeing her memories, fears. It was waiting, bored and hungry.
'Well?' a hiss said under something a bit like a bush.
'Yes …' she murmured, shaking. 'Yes, Miss I'm here.'

Charlotte Wood (12)
**The Becket School, Wilford**

# THE CHIP SHOP DISASTER

I walked into the chip shop. A man in front of me ordered chips and ketchup. It looked so tasty. I ordered the same. Before I knew it he chopped a child in half and fried the bones and put blood on top. I was shocked. The child was me.

Halyna Soltys (12)
**The Becket School, Wilford**

# UNTITLED

His van kept telling me to come here, but I couldn't. The man kept telling me to come here, but I walked. He shouted, 'Here, you can have some sweets!' I went over and said, 'Thank you.' I walked away but suddenly he grabbed me and that was game over.

Charlotte Johnston (12)
**The Becket School, Wilford**

# HOW TO LOOK HOT INSTEAD OF ROT

The teacher was very ugly and she wore green socks with orange boots and she wore a purple poncho. The children laughed at her, so she asked for advice and she changed her fashion sense. Then she turned very hot and when they looked, their mouths suddenly dropped!

Stephanie Gomes (12)

**The Becket School, Wilford**

# A DARK, DARK NIGHT

There was a young girl in a dark, dark room. She began to see the black shadow coming towards her. It was coming closer and closer. The girl was beginning to shake. Suddenly the lights turned on. Everything went very quiet. 'What would you like for tea?' said her mum.

Anna Lehane (12)

**The Becket School, Wilford**

# FINDING EMO

'Emo? Where are you? Emo?' Oh man I thought Emo had gone missing uh-gain! 'Emo! Damn it where are you?' It was snowing like mad! Oh man, it all started with that dodgy boy. I knew he was a bad influence. 'Emo! If you ...'
'I'm right here you know.'

Charles Denney (12)

**The Becket School, Wilford**

# THE SPORTS EQUIPMENT

One day out of the blue, when Jim went to the garage and picked up a football, he heard someone shout, 'Put me down!'
'Hey you! Come out wherever you are!' said Jim.
'I'm in your hands!' Jim looked down and saw the football
'Oh no, it can't be!'

Liam Haughney (11)

**The Becket School, Wilford**

# SNOW QUEEN

Snow started to fall, little did the Snow Queen know. The crispy, white snow fell faster like a heart beat. At the palace the Snow Queen's helper went out from her shift. She opened the door and saw it was snowing. She was excited, and shouted to the Snow Queen.

Alexandra Shelton-Bourke (12)

**The Becket School, Wilford**

# SHOPPING DISASTER

One day a mum was going shopping for food so she could eat dinner. She had to drive for 15 minutes. When she got to the supermarket she parked and got a trolley. When she got to the shopping centre doors a big explosion happened. Everyone died.

Shannon Anderson (11)

**The Becket School, Wilford**

# BEHIND CINDERELLA'S LIFE

Cinderella lived with her godmother and godsisters, forced to clean every day while her godmother was ill. Reading through the mail, she said, 'Cinderella, come here. It's an invitation to the ball.' In another room the sisters were going through their closet looking for an outfit for the ball.

Molly Edwards (12)

**The Becket School, Wilford**


# TV MADNESS

'I'm going to kill you, I'm going to rip your guts out and paint your house with them.'
'That's nothing compared to what I'm going to do to you. I'm going to tear your head off and raise it on a flag pole.'
'Chris turn the TV down.'
'Okay Mum.'

Liam Mackenzie (12)

**The Becket School, Wilford**

# UNTITLED

Today was a normal day, I mean normal because as the doorbell rang, I went to answer the door. But it was the Queen! So obviously she came in, sat herself down and I went to get some cuppas. Walking back in, I found my mates wetting themselves, 'April fools!'

Christopher Hannigan (12)

**The Becket School, Wilford**

# THE MISTAKE!

I stood there ... mouth wide open as I looked at this ginormous horrendous-looking shadow. 'Wait it ... it's a ... dinosaur.' It was coming towards me. Closer, closer, even closer. I could see now. It was a little boy in a costume. Well, it was Halloween of course.

Dominic Dowsett (12)

**The Becket School, Wilford**

## OH OH!

*Tap!* The office doors closed so quietly, that Lottie thought that the 'boss' hadn't heard. Looking around, Lottie saw blood grouped like lakes near her legs of the 'boss'. Lying unconscious was her, Mrs Yapy, the boss. Horrified, mouth open and scared, Lottie started screaming.

'Happy Halloween!' shouted Mrs Yapy.

Sherin Susan Roy (11)

**The Becket School, Wilford**

## DEATH!

*Bang!* The cold, cruel claws of death gripped the soul of poor, defenceless Andrew, who calmly welcomed the terrifying arms of death without a fuss, without a struggle ... *Bang!* Another grenade went off nearby, causing an extraordinary explosion and what seemed a horrific dream would soon become an unfortunate reality.

Alan Avery (12)

**The Becket School, Wilford**

## STUCK

I walked around my time machine, waiting. It felt different this time, maybe it had worked? I opened the door to see, what was the future! It'd worked! I walked out, ships were flying above me, it was amazing ... *Slam!* I turned to see my time machine flying off ... 'Noooo!'

Shannon Bull (12)

**The Becket School, Wilford**

## SPAM!

Days I've been searching the barren wasteland. Probing for human life. My mind is going mad, I can see a figure of a person walking on two legs! He's calling me over. I'd better go, he might have food and shelter. My final moments written deep inside an inky page.

Abigail Byrnes (11)

**The Becket School, Wilford**

# THE HAUNTING CONTINUED

During the days of dawn, there lived a boy named Kyle Cassat. He got bullied by the modern children, he got picked on, his books thrown to the ground. So progressing to the end of the day, he hanged himself... 18.26. Later that night, his haunting still continues ...

Matthew Nyatigi (12)

**The Becket School, Wilford**

# WATCH OUT DUCKY!

There was once a duck swimming alone happily in the lake. *Splash!* A wolf jumped in the water, trying to catch the duck for its dinner! The duck was terrified, not knowing what was happening! But unfortunately the wolf couldn't swim, so the duck swam off leaving the wolf alone!

Annabelle Earps (11)

**The Becket School, Wilford**

# FIREWORK

It darted through the air at full speed, swerving and spinning, just missing people's faces. 'Run!' People were screaming, running for their lives. People had no chance to miss this deadly weapon. Well that is what they thought. *Beep! Beep! Beep!* 'You've got to get up for school, hurry up!'

Cara Brown (11)

**The Becket School, Wilford**

# GOAL GLORY

He shot - *bang!* The ball flew into the net. The keeper had no chance. The home crowd cried, the away crowd flew up to rejoice. Jamie Beech had made it - one hat-trick for premier team Holy Spirit Celtic. Too bad those three goals were own goals!

Jamie Beech (11)

**The Becket School, Wilford**

# LIGHTNING

My limbs were frozen. I couldn't take my eyes off the lightning sparking from her fingertips, directed to me. My whole life flashed before my eyes: the people I'd loved and the adventures I'd had. But I did not fear death. I felt more alive then than I ever had.

Katie Booth (13)

**The Becket School, Wilford**

# IMPECCABLE TIMING

Clint Thrust heard his heartbeat. It was racing. The V12 engine howled as the back wheels slipped. His Aston was getting away from the two jet-black GTRs following him. The back window imploded. Clint drew his pistol and aimed ...
'Clint, time for tea,' Mum called. The PS3 went off.

Samuel Lawe (13)

**The Becket School, Wilford**

# RUNNING

I was running and panting so heavily you could hear me from Mars. It was no use. The darkened alley was closing in and I was never going to make it. The van was coming too quickly. I tripped into the van and it slammed shut. Where was I going?

Catherine Macarthur (13)

**The Becket School, Wilford**

# GONE

Her life had changed; her world gone. The waves had swallowed her life in one go. Her house was gone; her family was gone; her world was gone. Her livelihood turned upside down by nature. Nature - the monster and the friend. Nobody could forgive. The silent sea - guilty and sad.

Helen Dane (13)

**The Becket School, Wilford**

# LOST AND ALONE

The leaves blanketed the forest floor, as the petrified girl crept silently through the trees. Her teeth chattered and she blew hot air into her cupped hands. She didn't know where her family had vanished to. The wind whistled violently, causing the girl to shiver. She was lost and alone.

Rosy Patterson (13)

**The Becket School, Wilford**

# WHERE TO GO?
# WHAT TO DO?

Slowly, I awoke from a deep sleep, to a loud strange sound coming from the woods. Whilst approaching the woods, the sound stopped. Silence! On the other side of the woodlands, there were oval shaped flashing lights. It was a portal! I reached through. *Bang!* Where would I end up?

Luca Romano (11)

**The Becket School, Wilford**

# WHO'S AFRAID?

Little Red Riding Hood knocked at the door. She heard footsteps. The door opened in, on a house that smelled like old people. She looked at the figure in the nightie quickly. Small eyes, small ears and not a single tooth! It was Granny after all. Her heart sank deeply.

Niamh Williams (11)

**The Becket School, Wilford**

# THE DOOM OF THE DOG'S DINNER DASH

*Crash!* Ben raced at breakneck speed to avoid the oncoming plate that was hurling across the room towards him. He wished, *shouldn't have done my trick of eating my master's dinner again! Whack!* Ben hit the icy, brittle floor as a plate smashed onto his head. He lay limp … lifeless.

Evie Elizabeth Prest (11)

**The Becket School, Wilford**

# WILL YOU MARRY ME?

'Wow! I'm shocked. I mean, Buttons, nobody has ever been so nice to me before.'
'Yes but Cinderella, you have to answer my question. Will you marry me?'
'Fine, I'll answer your question.'
'Good,' said Buttons.
'But first, don't get mad if you don't like this. Well, here goes. I ...'

Kurdell Willis (11)

**The Becket School, Wilford**

# SNAIL-GASP

Antonio and Jane raced arrogantly to the finish line. *Crash!* As they smashed through the glass window of the Quickie-Mark. Then a giant snail popped out of nowhere and started licking everyone. It was like poison so it killed people. Antonio died and Jane stood with blank eyes - collapsed ...

Chitalu Chewe (11)

**The Becket School, Wilford**

# FRED THE DINOSAUR

Fred the dinosaur was a very happy dinosaur. He was a stegosaurus and extremely dumb! He was fiercely munching away at the grass after not eating for days, starving in the boiling desert. As he was chewing he heard a loud explosion and everything went black. His life had finished.

Sam Tomlinson (13)

**The Becket School, Wilford**

# UNTOUCHED MEMORIES

Sitting in his home, sorrowfully, the old man looked to his side where an empty chair lay. It still smelt of the person who once sat there, even though it had been untouched for many years. Breathing in the once familiar smell, he reminded himself that memories would always remain.

Lezia D'Souza (13)

**The Becket School, Wilford**

# NEVER WALK ALONE

Dark, cold, winter's night. As the young teenager was walking home he heard rustling in the bushes. He stopped, his heart racing. 'Who's there?' No answer. He called again, no response. He continued walking, weary of any danger until his dad suddenly jumped out; shouted, 'Gotcha!' The boy fell silent.

Chantelle Nicholson (13)

**The Becket School, Wilford**

# FORGET

Under the cherry tree with an incredible view of the town, is where he left me. As he left without saying another word, I cried with my heart torn into pieces. Years passed by and I started to change but he appeared again with a face that I didn't know.

Ythel Arimas (13)

**The Becket School, Wilford**

# THE SNIPER WHO LOST POWER

The detected sniper was now avoiding the enemy. He was being hit by his nerves, and the bullets. *Bang!* Now it was serious. The mines were hunting him as he was making his escape. Another bang! And now he lost it, the Xbox in his room had finally shut down.

Sergiy Bozhko (13)

**The Becket School, Wilford**

# A GORY DEATH

*Bang!* He was hurt. I knew I had to get help. He was bleeding badly. I sprinted as fast as I could to the telephone and dialled 999. The police arrived in seconds. I asked them if there was something they could do. They said no as he died slowly …

Alastair Tough (11)

**The Becket School, Wilford**

# MOOSE, WALRUS AND ME

We were in the classroom. Suddenly there was an ear-screeching noise. Mrs Quirk was turning into a moose! We all screamed in horror. She began to eat paper and break tables! Then Conor turned into a walrus! Oh no - next was me! 'Argh! Help!' I screamed, petrified. 'Help!' ...

Kieran Whittaker (12)

**The Becket School, Wilford**

# THE GAME OF MY LIFE

This was it - winning was essential. Whewww! The game started; it was all very close. Suddenly the ball came to him. He controlled it and tapped into an unbreakable sprint. He took on one player, then the next. *Boom!* He shot - it ripped the net. Then it was all over.

Noah Denzil de Sousa (11)

**The Becket School, Wilford**

# THE CRIMINAL CAPERS
# OF THE KILLER CAT!

This is the record of my criminal capers. I was involved in bunny butchery and cod catching. My first crimes were actual birdily harm and pilchard pilfery. My most recent crime was assault and cattery. I'm part of the Sharpened Claws Organization, aiming to bring down the Ministry of Moggies.

Hannah Parr (11)

**The Becket School, Wilford**

# JANE BULLY-ME AND
# WHAT SHE DID NEXT!

Jane Bully-Me was a girl who was always bullied, just because of her name. So she wished on a star and out came a big bright light. Jane was amazed and walked towards the light, then she was in a beautiful place. She lived there for the rest of time ...

Mia Ruby Cleugh (11)

**The Becket School, Wilford**

# MY LAST DIARY ENTRY
# RON WEASLEY

Dear Diary,
The day Harry entered my compartment: life changed.
Least loved by my mother. I left and came back. Brother
dead, Hermione hugging me. Harry victorious. All is
well and on my deathbed writing this, praying for my
children. I'm scared, look after my family old friend,
Ron Weasley.

Laura Burke (11)

**The Becket School, Wilford**

# THE BIG BLACK CAT

*Whoosh!* It ran past like a bolt of black lightning with
sharp teeth. Then it stopped and turned to face me, its
eyes slits in a pool of green fire. Suddenly it charged
head first at me. I just dodged it. But the monster wasn't
as lucky. *Bang!* It fell …

Bailey Swan (11)

**The Becket School, Wilford**

# A MUSHROOM'S POINT OF VIEW

I blame my parents, for me being a mushroom! We're meant to be fungi. Those scientists think they know everything but they don't! Those humans also think they can just walk all over us - literally! Oh, here comes another one of those stupid humans, coming to investigate me again, *again* ...

Caoilainn Daragh Rhodes (11)
**The Becket School, Wilford**

# DOG'S PLANE ADVENTURE PART I

There was a dog. The dog was called Dog. Dog was going to Antarctica to meet the penguin king who was called King P. Dog's plane crashed on Madagascar. Dog found monkeys to fix the plane. The monkeys wanted to steal the plane. The king got his rocket to kill Dog ...

Sean Burrows (11)
**The Becket School, Wilford**

# THE FOOTBALL MATCH

World Cup final, here I am. Last five minutes. The score is 0-0. The ball flies through the air towards me. It bounces just in front of me. What a tight angle, but I have to shoot. It's crazy! It's in! Yes! The crowd goes wild! Then I wake up.

Daniel Cawley (12)

**The Becket School, Wilford**

# THE SCARECROW GOES TO THE PETROL STATION

The scarecrow jumped off his sticks and climbed over his hedge! He was in his scaretruck going to the petrol station. Scarecrow said in a normal way, 'Fill him up.'
'Oh right, here you go!'
'Thanks,' said Scarecrow He jumped on his sticks and went to sleep. 'Good bye,' he whispered.

Kieran Lawton (11)

**The Becket School, Wilford**

# THE STATION

Peter stepped in front of the platform. He wanted to be at peace, alone. 'Don't go, Pete! Please!' He turned around. A girl with blonde hair was standing there.
'I have to do this, Daisy,' Peter said, calmly. He looked back one final time, longing for no more; and leaped.

Joseph Blomefield (11)

**The Becket School, Wilford**

# THE GIRL WHO DIED
# AND CAME BACK TO LIFE
# IN NEVERING LAND

There lived a girl called Desting. Desting lived in a land called Nevering Land. Nevering Land was in the south of Nottingham. Desting lived with her mum. Desting's brother died in a car crash with his dad. Desting and her mum worked all night to keep alive or die.

Favour Odiogor-Odoh (12)

**The Becket School, Wilford**

# EVIL ERICA

Evil Erica watched her screen. Five, four, three, two, one. A steel foot came round the corner, squashing a new Senetra. Greg the Good, who was sworn to protect the city, was nowhere in sight. He was chained up, watching his city die.

Eleanor Stiles (12)

**The Becket School, Wilford**

# THE SNOW

I could smell the bitter aroma of sadness in the atmosphere. My feet were as cold as icebergs. The snow ripped out my heart and my soul. It dropped down like teardrops around my fat cheeks. 'Snow!' This (word) reminded me of war. The 'snow' was my enemy.

Devni Edirisinghe (11)

**The Becket School, Wilford**

# THE MURDERER

Once upon a time there was a murderer called Bob. He was wanted for shooting and knifing people in the head. The police had been searching for him for days but finally they found him in an abandoned warehouse. When the police found him they shot him in the head.

Patrick Ferguson (11)

**The Becket School, Wilford**

# SATISFACTION

It sang with its small guitar, moving to the rhythm. The frog danced as its webbed feet tapped to the beat. Behind it a large bird approached without a sound. As quick as a flash, a crash of a beak, and the bird was satisfied.

Lucy Cockburn (11)

**The Becket School, Wilford**

## HOLIDAY HAUNTS

Imagine an ugly haunted house in the heart of a forbidden forest. A shimmering light in the attic shows a faded silhouette gliding gently to the right. Shattered windowpanes leave a jaw for uninvited guests to die with pain. *Great holiday cottage* thought the Grim Reaper. *Let's book it.*

Lawrence Cotter (11)

**The Becket School, Wilford**


## DEATH

Death is calling as I walk up to John's grave. Wind cuts through my body, ringing throughout my ears. I can feel his presence reaching into my soul. A clot in my heart, a lump in my throat. 'John, leave me! I regret killing you that night. I miss you.'

Hannah Barry (12)

**The Brunts School, Mansfield**

# GEORGE AND THE DRAGON

George stared at the dragon's grotesque features. Smoke curled up from its flaring nostrils and its body was smothered in thousands of spines. Monstrous teeth protruded from its massive jaws and it was guarding a princess. Suddenly the dragon faded and he heard his teacher saying, 'George! Stop daydreaming now!'

Jacob Evans (12)

**The Brunts School, Mansfield**

# JASPER THE DOG

*Grr that stupid boy!* Jasper the dog pondered, he hadn't been fed for days now and he was ravenous! Suddenly he had an idea ... So he crept out of his basket and into Maxwell's room. Doggedly, he leapt up onto the desk and gobbled up his homework!

Kieran Boardman (11)

**The Brunts School, Mansfield**

# SPECIAL FRIENDS

There was once a little fish called Jimmy. One day Jimmy was trapped by Bob the seal, who was a bully to Jimmy. Suddenly Jimmy's special friend, the great white shark, glided swiftly in the water and frightened Bob away. Jimmy realised how good it was to have special friends.

Thomas Bryan (12)

**Wilsthorpe Community School, Long Eaton**

# A CLEVER COW

Jack had no money and was forced to sell his prized cow Daisy. On the high street he sold her, and was sad. On the way home he found her abandoned. She'd pretended to be ill. Jack was happy, he had his money and Daisy. His mum would be proud!

Alice Burton (13)

**Wilsthorpe Community School, Long Eaton**

# THE FOREST MONSTER

Jack was trekking through the forest. It smelt damp as he cut his way through the bushes. Suddenly out of nowhere, a monster lashed out, with its huge teeth and bare hands. The creature tore at everything. He stopped it with his trap, he'd saved the forest and was alive!

Daniel Trueman (12)

**Wilsthorpe Community School, Long Eaton**

# THE HORROR HOUSE

There it stood - the deserted horror house. The wind howled, while the roof timbers fell, leaving the gaunt roof timbers like a skeleton beneath flesh. Joe wearily entered, fearing for his life ... Would he ever leave alive ... ? The coffin awaited.

Leah Collins (12)

**Wilsthorpe Community School, Long Eaton**

# DETENTION

*I need to get home* I thought to myself. *I can't go to my detention after school, Mum will kill me.* Soon as the bell went I ran home. When I got home, the phone rang. Mum said on the phone, 'Wilsthorpe?' She turned and looked at me ...

Grace Phipps (11)

**Wilsthorpe Community School, Long Eaton**

# THE FISH WHO NEARLY LOST HER BEST FRIEND

Jane wanted to live at the top of the reef. She thought she had nothing. But she was wrong. There was her best friend called Jake. Then everyone found out about her lie. She went to the bottom. She realised that her best friend was hard to get back.

Leah Haynes (11)

**Wilsthorpe Community School, Long Eaton**

# SUNSHINE THE PIXIE

There once was a pixie called Sunshine with hair as gold as the sunset, and eyes as blue as sapphires. Sunshine was always left out of everything and was always picked last. Some candles came under her door. She wished on one and she was popular.

Emily Tomlinson (11)
**Wilsthorpe Community School, Long Eaton**

# THE NIGHT THAT WAS A NIGHTMARE

*Smash!* Why did the door slam? I put my dressing gown on and ran down the stairs. On the floor was some red stuff, was it blood? Who knew. Then from nowhere a voice said, 'Let's play a game.' I turned around and standing there was a huge masked figure ...

Mitchell Werezak (11)
**Wilsthorpe Community School, Long Eaton**

# YOUNG WRITERS
## INFORMATION

We hope you have enjoyed reading this book - and that you will continue to enjoy it in the coming years.
If you like reading and creative writing drop us a line, or give us a call, and we'll send you a free information pack.

Alternatively if you would like to order further copies of this book or any of our other titles, then please give us a call or log onto our website at **www.youngwriters.co.uk**

Young Writers Information
Remus House
Coltsfoot Drive
Peterborough
PE2 9BF
Tel: (01733) 890066